For Moira

Your shining smile and unique sincerity make the world a brighter place
You inspire me beyond my limits
I love you very, very much

Daddy PiMM

First published in Belgium and Holland by Clavis Uitgeverij, Hasselt – Amsterdam, 2013
Copyright © 2013, Clavis Uitgeverij

English translation from the Dutch by Clavis Publishing Inc. New York
Copyright © 2014 for the English language edition: Clavis Publishing Inc. New York

Visit us on the web at www.clavisbooks.com

A *Tummy Full of Secrets* written by Pimm van Hest and illustrated by Nynke Talsma
Original title: *Een buik vol geheimen*
Translated from the Dutch by Clavis Publishing

ISBN 978-1-60537-201-3

This book was printed in September 2014 at Proost Industries N.V., Everdongenlaan 23, 2300 Turnhout, Belgium

First Edition
10 9 8 7 6 5 4 3 2 1

A Tummy Full of Secrets

Pimm van Hest & Nynke Talsma

Clavis
NEW YORK

My name is *Moira*.

My mommy and daddy are the best in the whole wide world!

We have two funny dogs called Zorro and Splinter.

Every now and then I am a bit clumsy and sometimes a bit naughty.

I can also be a bit headstrong.

"That's okay," says Mommy.

But sometimes it can be pretty annoying too.

Especially when I don't want to or don't dare to talk about things.

Like yesterday.

I woke up at seven am.
Rise and shine!
Out of bed, and getting dressed.
Everything went fine until I saw a small thread
hanging from my tights.
I tugged at it ever so gently,
and a small hole appeared.
I tugged again.

Suddenly,

ZZZZZZZZZ

$ziiiiiiiiiippppp$

the hole got bigger.

Oh no, what to do?

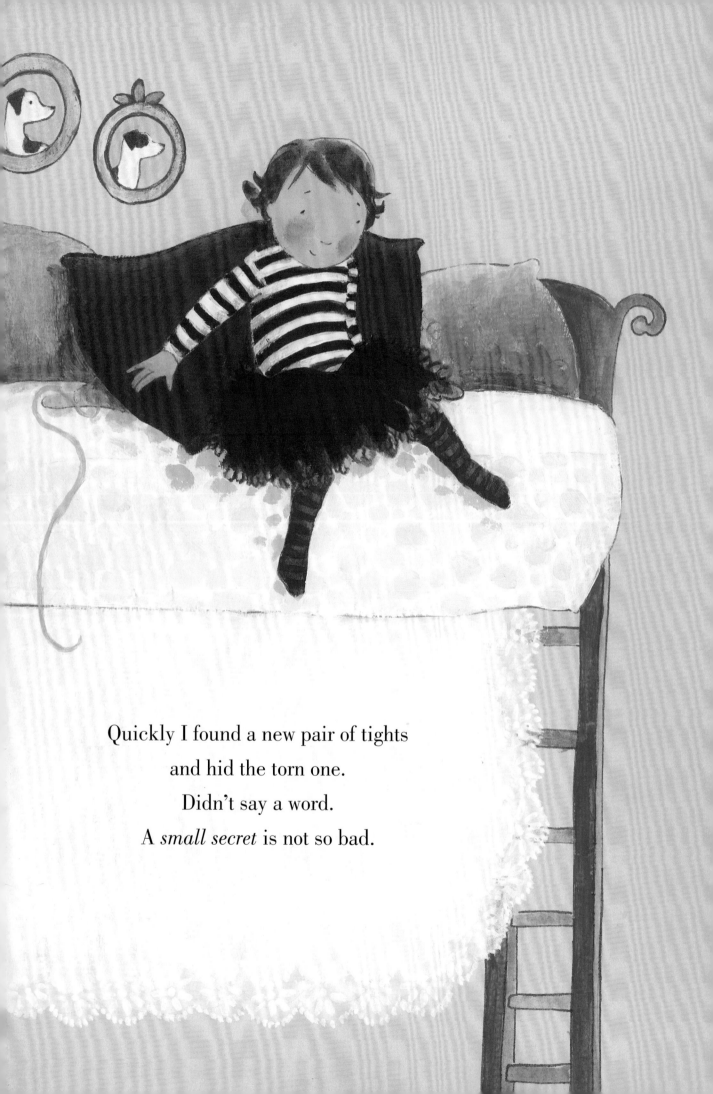

Quickly I found a new pair of tights
and hid the torn one.
Didn't say a word.
A *small secret* is not so bad.

"*Hey,*" Mommy said, "*a different pair of tights.*
This one looks good too."
I wanted to tell her.
I even felt the words tickling in my throat.
But I swallowed and

WHOOPs

They slid back into my tummy.
They would be safe there. Or so I thought.

At school it was all I could think of.
I knew Mommy wouldn't be happy with a
pair of ripped tights.
She always says: *"Look after your clothes
and don't pick at the threads!"*

When I tried to eat my fruit in class,
I felt my tummy *tickle*.
My tummy didn't feel like eating a pear,
and neither did I.
So I put my pear back in my bag.

After school Benjamin walked home
with me. He was coming over to play.
When we were almost home,
I suddenly remembered the pear.
I also thought of Daddy. He says:
"Always eat your fruit, Moira.
Vitamins are your best friends!"
Daddy will probably be angry when he
sees the pear in my bag, I thought.
Do you want to know what I did?
I took the pear and threw it in the bin.

"How was your day, Sweetheart?"
Daddy asked when we came in.
I almost opened my mouth to tell Daddy about
the tights and the pear.
But I heard Benjamin calling.
"Moira, come quickly, I have a brilliant idea."

So I pushed the *little secrets* back into my tummy.
Room enough down there.
I'll tell him some other time.

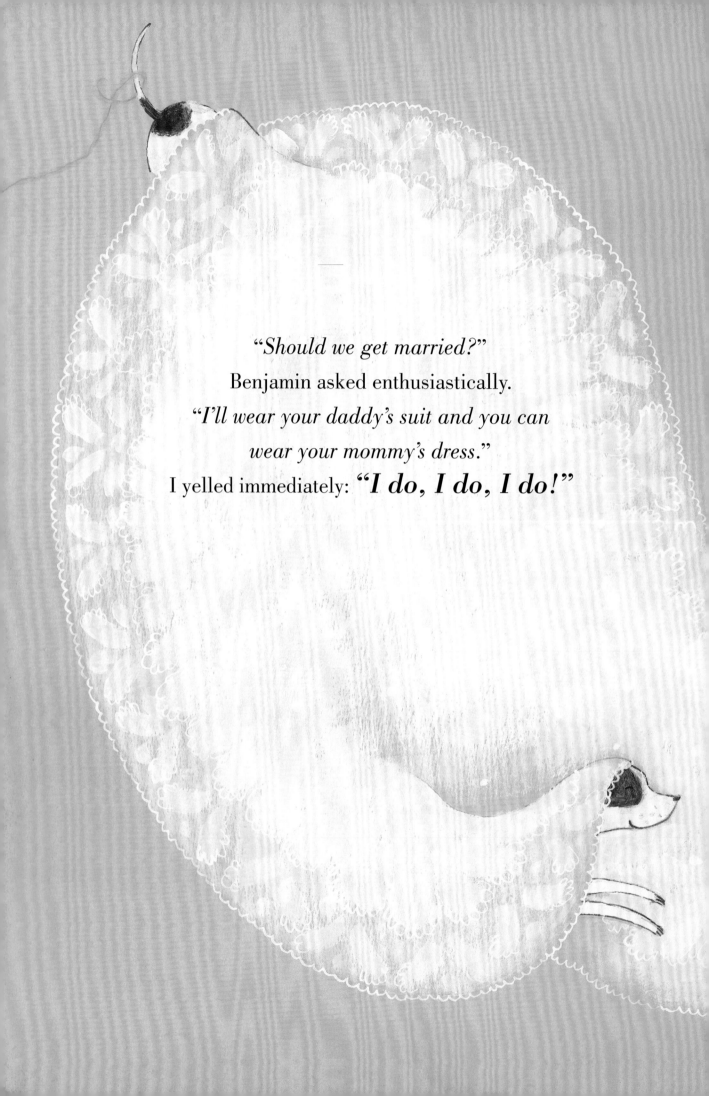

"*Should we get married?*"
Benjamin asked enthusiastically.
"*I'll wear your daddy's suit and you can*
wear your mommy's dress."
I yelled immediately: "**I do, I do, I do!**"

Of course the dress was *far too big*
and the train was very very long.
But, boy, did I look pretty.
Benjamin looked a bit like a penguin wearing
a jacket that was far too big.
During the wedding ceremony I suddenly had to pee.
Really, really suddenly.

I ran and stumbled into the bathroom
and sat down on the toilet seat.

psssssh

psSSSsh

psssssh

that was a big pee.

I only noticed it when I got up. ***Oh no!***
I had peed all over the train. What a disaster.
I took off the dress in a panic
and hung it back inside the closet.
I asked Benjamin to go home.
The wedding was over.

When Mommy came home from work
she gave me a kiss and a hug.
"It's so nice to be home again," she said.
"We'll have dinner in fifteen minutes."
I wanted to tell Mommy about the dress, but I just couldn't.
This was so terrible. Mommy would surely be very sad.
And I also felt slightly ashamed.
So I put *this third little secret* in my tummy as well.
I sensed that my tummy was almost *full*.

Dinner was a disaster!
I could only just swallow the soup,
but could not manage the meat at all.
I chewed and chewed....

I chewed...

and chewed....

chommmmm

chommmmm..

My tummy was filled with *secrets* and the words to tell
about them were stuck in my throat.
I secretly gave my food to our dogs Zorro and Splinter.
I even skipped dessert.
After dinner I went straight to my room.

Sadly I sat down on my bed. I didn't feel well at all.
I had a *tummy ache* and didn't know what to do.

Tiptap, tiptap, tiptap

and

step, step, step

"Tell us, Sweetheart, what's going on?"
Kindly and gently Mommy put her hand on my tummy.
I couldn't keep *the secrets* hidden any longer.
They all came out at the same time.

I pulled a hole in my tights,

and I threw my pear in the bin,

and I accidentally peed all over the train of your wedding dress,

and I secretly gave my dinner to Zorro and Splinter....

"Well, that must be a relief, Sweetheart," Mommy said.

Daddy put his arm around me and said: *"Sweetie, you know you can always tell us everything. We may be a bit mad or sad, but we'll always love you very much."*

"And you know what," Mommy said,
"we'll be really sad if you have to walk around with a tummy full of secrets."
She winked at me, and Daddy gave me a big kiss.
When all my tears had dried, the secrets were gone.
"Maybe there's still room for delicious dessert?" asked Mommy.

And you know what?
It was the **best dessert**
I have ever had!